2B

My D

MY DAD
A PICTURE CORGI BOOK 978 0 552 56006 1

First published in Great Britain by Doubleday,
an imprint of Random House Children's Publishers UK
A Random House Group Company

Doubleday edition published 2000
Picture Corgi edition published 2001
This edition published 2010

19

Designed by Ian Butterworth

Picture Corgi Books are published by Random House Children's Publishers UK,
61–63 Uxbridge Road, London W5 5SA

www.**randomhousechildrens**.co.uk

Addresses for companies within The Random House Group Limited
can be found at: www.randomhouse.co.uk/offices.htm

THE RANDOM HOUSE GROUP Limited Reg. No. 954009

A CIP catalogue record for this book is available from the British Library

Printed in China

Anthony Browne

Picture Corgi

He's all right, my dad.

My dad isn't afraid of ANYTHING,

even the Big Bad Wolf.

He can jump right over the moon,

and walk on a tightrope (without falling off).

He can wrestle with giants,

or win the fathers' race on
sports day, easily.

He's all right, my dad.

My dad can eat like a horse,

and he can swim like a fish.

He's as strong as a gorilla,

and as happy as a hippopotamus.

He's all right, my dad.

My dad's as big as a house,

and as soft as my teddy.

He's as wise as an owl,

and daft as a brush.

He's all right, my dad.

My dad's a great dancer,

and a brilliant singer.

He's fantastic at football,

and he makes me laugh. A lot.

I love my dad.
And you know what?

HE LOVES ME!

(And he always will.)

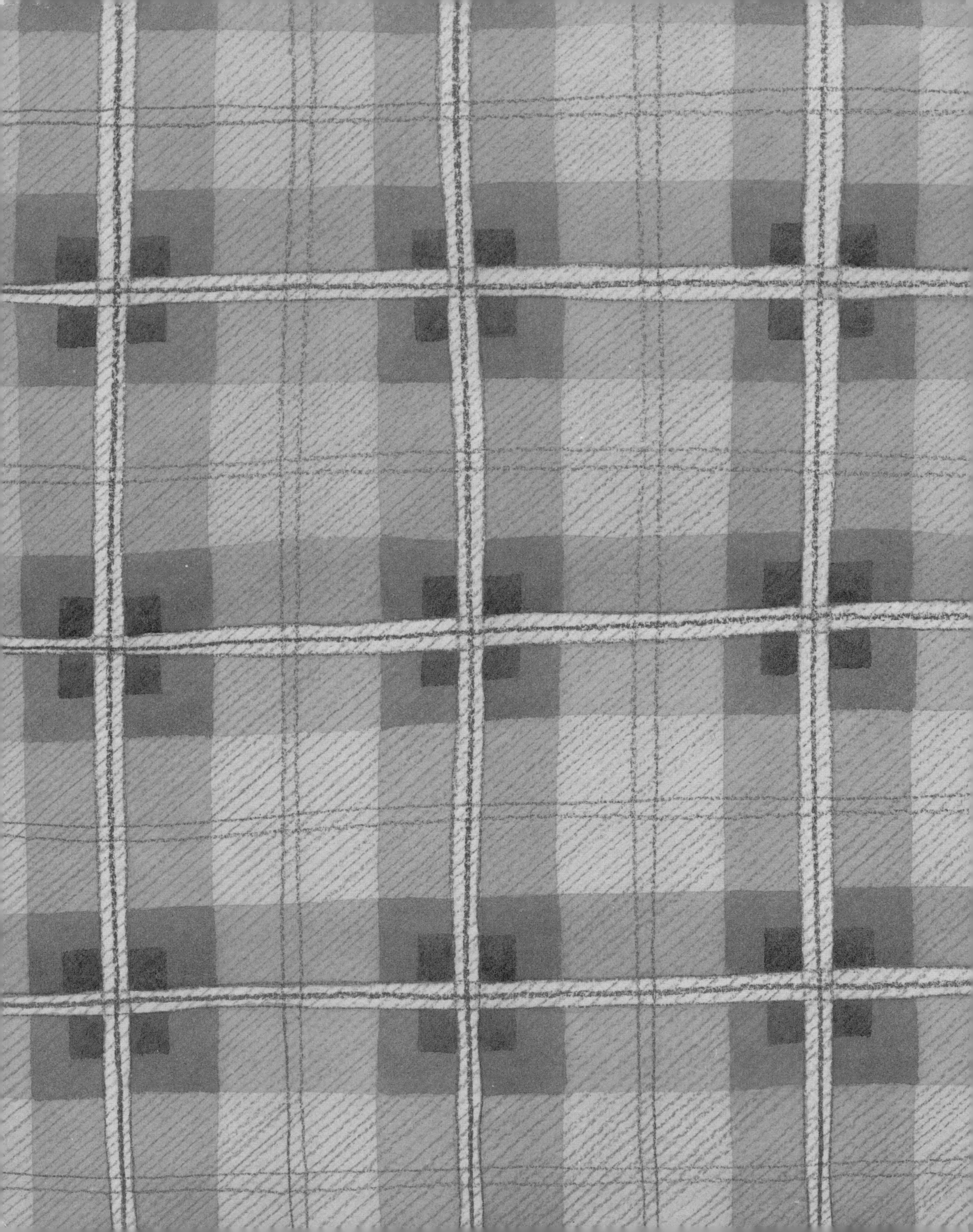